To LOON LAKE
and all my family and friends
who ran in her woods and swam
in her cool water.

VIKING
Penguin Young Readers
An imprint of Penguin Random House LLC
375 Hudson Street
New York, New York 10014

First published in the United States of America by Viking,
an imprint of Penguin Random House LLC, 2018

Copyright © 2018 by David Covell

LIBRARY OF CONGRESS CATALOGING-IN-PUBLICATION DATA IS AVAILABLE.
ISBN 9780670014118
Special Markets ISBN 9781984837103 Not for Resale

Printed in China

1 3 5 7 9 10 8 6 4 2

This Imagination Library edition is published by Penguin Young Readers, a division
of Penguin Random House, exclusively for Dolly Parton's Imagination Library,
a not-for-profit program designed to inspire a love of reading and learning, sponsored
in part by The Dollywood Foundation. Penguin's trade editions of this work are
available wherever books are sold.

Run Wild

DAVID COVELL

VIKING

Sprout, you're out!

Crunch. Crack. Twig. SNAP!

Squeaky clean?
Who cares about that?

Squish. Fiddlehead.

Squirm. Fern,

Meet a beetle.
Talk to worms.

Are you brave?
Come on, explore...

Faster, feet!
On to the shore.

Hot!
HOT!
Burning
sand.

Ahhhh...
Cool.
Hello,
Clam.

Take a deep breath.
1-2-3!

Be a fish in
the salty sea.

Now, UP for air!

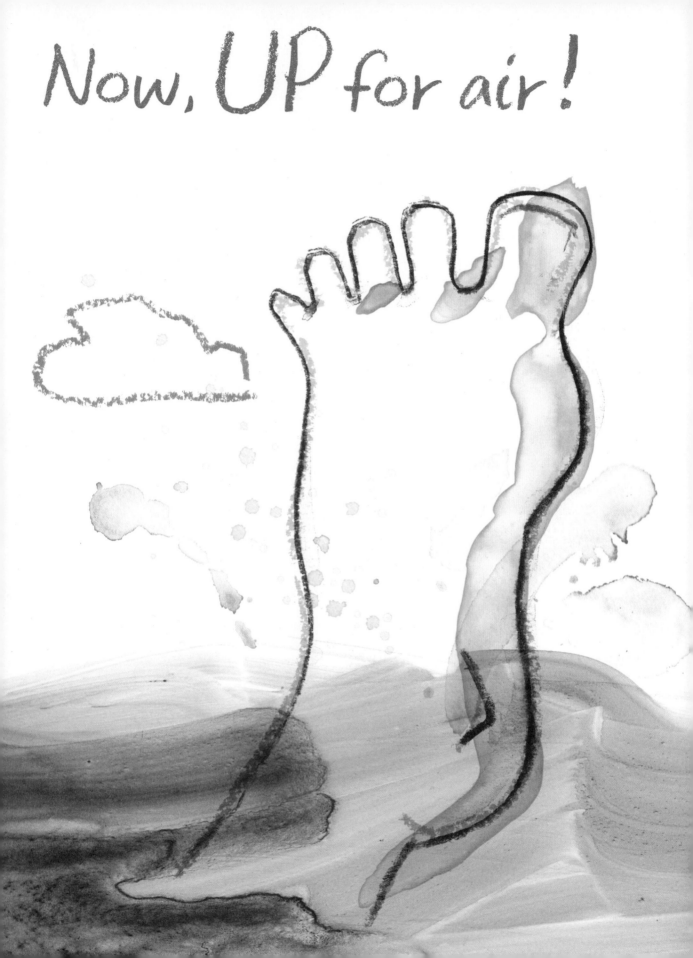

Just float there....

Waves. Rolling.
Daydreams. Flowing.

What's next,
you wonder?

Run! Run!
Wild. Wild.
Some days the sun
<u>WON'T</u> smile.

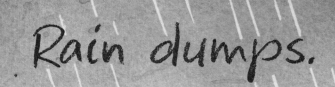

Rain dumps.

There'll be
slippery slumps.

Bruises.
Bumps . . .

and ROTTEN STUMPS!

ugh.

slug.

Are you okay?
I think so.

Come on, then.
Let's keep going.

Breeze. Blowing.

Sunset. Glowing.

"Ah-woooo

Moon's gonna smile.
Run. Run.
Wild.
Wild.

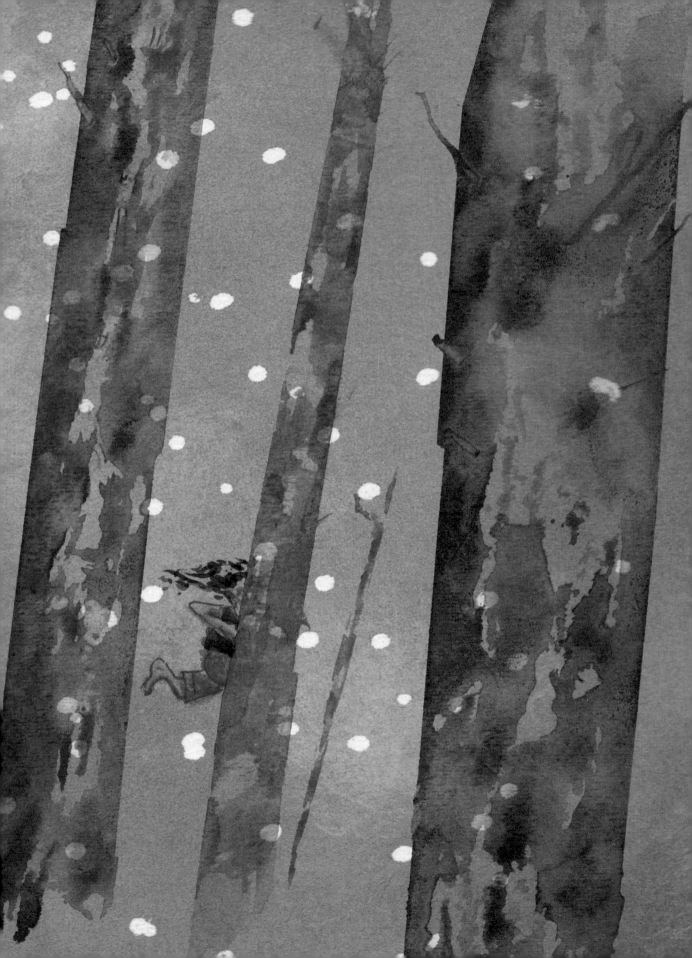